GATO

Margaret Elphinstone

QUICK & EASY

BBC

LARGE
PRINT

First published in 2005 by
Sandstone Press
This Large Print edition published
2007 by BBC Audiobooks
by arrangement with
Sandstone Press Ltd

ISBN 978 1 405 62222 6

British Library Cataloguing in Publication Data available

Printed and bound in Great Britain by
Antony Rowe Ltd., Chippenham, Wiltshire

GATO

Gato is the story of a young child brought up in a mill. The quiet hardworking lives of the people at the mill are disturbed by the arrival of a wandering Spanish Friar. What is going on between the miller and his wife, and the Friar? The child at the centre of the story tries to understand. The only creatures the child is close to are the mill cats. After the Friar's stay, there is always one called Gato, Spanish for 'cat'.

To Ginger and all the other cats

CHAPTER ONE

Sit down. It's been a busy day. Did you want to see Joan? She's in the mill, talking to Tom, the merchant's son. That's Tom's cart out there in the yard, with the big dapple grey horses. He came over today with another cart full of grain. The last load of corn he brought has all been ground into flour. Soon we'll be loading up the sacks of flour for him to take back to the town. But we'll have our dinner first. We'll eat as soon as Tom's finished talking business with Joan, and they come in from the mill.

This is the time of year when everyone comes to the mill. The corn has been harvested, and all the fields are bare. Sometimes the farmers bring their own grain. Often, though, the grain comes from the corn merchant in the town. Tom brings it over in that big cart. Those two horses of Tom's are twice as tall as my cousin Joan. Tom keeps the horses well groomed. He combs out their manes and tails, and their hairy fetlocks. He polishes their harness until it shines. Tom looks very fine sitting up there above his horses, driving the huge cart. These days he wears a sprig of blue cornflower in his cap.

Each time Tom comes with the cart full of grain, he sits here in our kitchen for a long time. He talks to my cousin Joan. I hate that. I hate it when he sits so long at our table when dinner is finished. I hate the way he looks at Joan while he speaks. There is a warm look in his eyes that speaks to me of danger. I wish Tom would not come.

There are just the three of us here at the mill now: my Aunt Edith, my cousin Joan, and me. We are happy enough. Nothing has changed for a long time. I don't want change. I have seen too many changes.

When I say nothing has changed, I realise that is not true. Joan has changed. I have seen her grow from a baby to a little girl, and from a little girl into a young woman. Her father, my Uncle Garth the Miller, was a big tall man, but Joan is small and slight. Her eyes are so dark brown that in some lights they seem black. Her hair is black too, but when she is at work in the mill she ties a scarf round her head, and her long hair is hidden. I only see Joan's hair on Saturday nights, when she takes off her scarf and combs out her hair for Sunday. Although Joan's hair is as black as night, the firelight brings out red lights in it. It gleams in the light of the flames. I watch her thin brown hands moving up and down as she combs her hair. Joan doesn't look strong enough to lift a tray of loaves off the griddle, let alone a big sack of flour or a hod of grain. But Joan is stronger than she looks. She is tough, and she works beside me all day in the mill. She's not as strong as I am, of course, but she can work just as hard, and for just as long, as I do.

I wish Joan had a father to look after her. Aunt Edith is a good mother, I suppose. I think Aunt Edith likes Tom. Aunt Edith always invites Tom to sit down and eat with us before he goes back to the town. Aunt Edith won't tell Joan what to do. Joan has a stronger will than her mother. But I remember when Aunt Edith had a will of her own, and showed it, too.

You never knew Edith when she was young. No doubt you think of her as just an old widow woman. That's what she looks like now. She doesn't work in the mill. She never did. She was never strong enough for that. But when I was a child I feared the sound of her scolding, and the weight of her hand too. I suppose she did her best to be kind to me. She didn't want me, but I was here before she came, and there was nothing she could do about that. She wouldn't have dared to ask my Uncle Garth to send me away. No, I was part of the mill, and even when she was a spoiled young bride she had to accept me.

Garth thought the world of Edith. She was the prettiest girl in this valley. Everyone thought it was a very good match. She had a temper though. Those cold eyes that look at you now—I can remember when they would flash with rage. I knew when I had to keep out of her way. But then I've always been good at keeping out of the way.

But what was it you were asking me about? Gato, that was it. You asked why the tom cat at the mill has always been called Gato. Well, I'll tell you. It goes right back to when I was a little child. It goes back to the time that the Spanish Friar first came to our mill. Do you want me to tell you the whole story?

CHAPTER TWO

I was eight years old when the Spanish Friar came to our mill. I didn't know what a Friar was, so I asked my Aunt Edith what the strange word meant. 'A Friar is a holy man,' she said. 'A Friar loves God and is kind to the poor. He has made a vow that he will always be poor himself. He will travel the world as a pilgrim, and go to all the holy places he can get to. He will be kind to everyone he meets, rich or poor. He has given away all that he owns so that he can help others.'

I thought about what Aunt Edith said. I knew that I would much rather not be poor, and not have to walk the dusty roads in all weathers. I didn't want to wear a brown robe and sandals all my life, to show that I didn't care about having my own things. I would rather stay at the mill, and keep warm in winter, and stay indoors when it rained or snowed. I would rather have proper clothes to wear, and shoes on my feet. I would rather have a home and not have to travel to strange countries in all seasons and weathers. But at the same time I wanted more than anything else to be like the Spanish Friar. From the day that I first set eyes on him, he was my idea of what a man should be.

I was sitting on the wooden stair that leads up to the mill when the Friar first knocked at the gate. Edith went to open it.

'Can I help you?' she asked.

'Yes,' said the Spanish Friar. 'I am a pilgrim. I have come from the Holy Shrine of the Blessed Virgin Mary. I am tired and hungry. Will you, out of the kindness of your heart, give me some food? Will you let me stay the night here at your mill? I think it will rain, and I would like to have a dry bed.'

I had never before heard anyone speak like the Spanish Friar. In his mouth the hard sounds of our English words sounded softer and thicker. Hearing his voice was like listening to a song. I wasn't used to hearing much talk. When my Uncle Garth and I worked in the mill we hardly spoke because of the noise of rushing water and grinding mill stones. In the evening when the mill was quiet Garth was still a man of few words. I have never learned to chat, or tell stories. But from the moment that the Spanish Friar first spoke to us, I wanted to hear him talk. I wanted to find out all that he had to say.

I had seen beggars come to our door before. Aunt Edith always sent them away. Most beggars would be lucky to get a crust of bread from her. But she didn't send away the Spanish Friar. I suppose this was

9

because he was a holy man. But when she first spoke kindly to him, I was very surprised.

'You are welcome,' said Aunt Edith. She held the gate open. 'Come in, and I will find some food.'

The Friar stepped through the open gate and into the yard. One of the kittens ran out from the mill door, and raced sideways across the yard. It got caught up in the Friar's brown robe. The Friar tripped. Edith grabbed his arm to keep him from falling. For a moment he held her arm, and laughed.

'O, *el gato*!'

That was the first Spanish word I ever heard. *Gato* means *cat*. Ever since the Friar came, we have always had a cat called Gato at the mill.

Later on the Friar taught me more Spanish words: *el molino*—the mill, *la mujer*—the woman, *agua*—water. I have never used those words again, but I can remember them as well as ever.

CHAPTER THREE

At the time the Friar came, Edith
had been married to my uncle the
miller for three years. My uncle did
not suit her, but the mill did. From
the moment that Edith stepped into
the mill, it fitted her, like a sheath
fits the knife that's made for it. It
wasn't her mill, though. The mill
belonged to my Uncle Garth. His
father and his grandfather had been
millers there before him. The
millers' wives were nobodies. They
were just girls from the farms, and no
one remembered their names. But
everyone remembers Garth the
Miller's name. My uncle and my
grandfather and my great-
grandfather were all called Garth. I
wonder what they think now, those
dead men, when they see that the

miller now is not a son but a daughter? After all those men came a slip of a girl. But I have not come to Joan yet. I'm still telling you about the arrival of the Spanish Friar.

I had never seen a man like the Spanish Friar. The first evening he was here, we sat in the yard in the last of the sun. My hands were stained purple from picking brambles. I'd been out in the fields all day, searching the hedges. As I'd walked, hips and brambles and the last of the honeysuckle towered above me. The sun touched their tops, while I stood in the shadows below. I was small for my age, and, as I told you, I can't have been more than eight years old.

Twenty-three years have gone by since the Spanish Friar came to our gate. I can still see him in my mind. He looked like Joan would look, if she were a man, and if she were ten years older than she is now. He had thick dark hair, and where it was shaved on top it was already growing back like fur. He had dark eyes like Joan's. Everyone says Joan's eyes are like her mother's. That's not true. You look at Joan and Aunt Edith, the next time you catch them sitting side by side. It's true that they both have brown eyes, but they're not the same kind of brown. Edith's hair was fair—well, it was more mouse colour really. People would call it fair if they were being polite. Her hair was fair—now it's grey—and it was very curly. She has brown eyes that look at you hard, though to tell the truth she's usually only thinking that you should brush your hair another way, or wash the stains from round your mouth.

But look at Edith and Joan, next time they're sitting side by side. They often do, you know. They sit on the bench by the kitchen table. They work together like sisters. Yesterday they were shelling beans. They had two piles of beans and one bowl between them. The neighbours were all in there drinking their ale and watching Edith and Joan. But no one sees what I see, ever.

Joan's eyes? Yes, they're brown, it's true, but they're a deep dark brown, like the space between things. When you look into the wood in winter, the birch trees are purple in the dusk. Behind them the trees fade away into—what? It's not the hill you're seeing. It's not the sky. It's the dark creeping into the space waiting for it, once the sun has set. Joan wouldn't be looking at stains round your mouth or uncombed hair, but I never knew such a girl for finding what no one else sees.

Mushrooms, for example—she's good at finding mushrooms. She came back yesterday with a basket full of different kinds of mushroom. The strange brown and orange shapes in her basket gleamed in the dusk like fishes in the stream.

The Friar used to collect golden

mushrooms for us too. He had a word for them: *chanterelles*. He said they grew in Spain as well. He'd come back from the woods, and bring mushrooms and berries and hazel nuts, whatever he'd found. In Spain, he said, he'd have had sweet chestnuts and walnuts too. When he talked of his home he seemed to be gazing past me at something I could not see. I thought maybe it was Spain he was looking at.

It was my Uncle Garth who invited the Spanish Friar to stay as long as he wished. Edith didn't say much the first night that the Friar was with us. After a while she went indoors to cook our meal. Garth asked the Friar about his travels. I knew Edith was listening. The kitchen window stood open and I could smell mutton and herbs from the cooking. The Friar had a big flat shell at his belt. I came closer so I could look at it.

The Friar smiled at me kindly. 'Are you looking at my shell? That's a scallop shell. I wear it at my belt because I've visited a Holy Shrine in Spain. It's the shrine of Saint James, at a place with a Spanish name: *Compostella*. Every pilgrim who goes to Compostella wears a scallop shell to show that they have been there.'

My uncle said, 'Did you travel a long way to go to that shrine?'

'On no,' said the Spanish Friar. 'I started from there. I come from the mountains near Compostella. When I was a young man I thought it was wrong that my family had a good farm and plenty of money, when there were many people in the world who had nothing. I saw children begging for food in the streets, and old people cast out by their families to die on the road. I thought that was wrong. God asks us to be kind to one another, and I did not see the people around me being kind, or fair. So I walked from my home to the shrine of St. James to find the Friars. That was how I set out on the path of a pilgrim. Since then I've walked the length of Europe and beyond. I've been to the Holy City of Jerusalem, and I've stayed among the infidels as I stay among you now.'

'What's an infidel?' I hardly spoke above a whisper because I was very shy. But I wanted to know so badly that I dared to speak to him.

'An infidel is someone who is not Christian. The Arabs who live in Jerusalem are all infidels. They believe in a God called Allah, and they don't believe that Jesus was the Son of God.' The Friar glanced at my Uncle Garth as if he wasn't sure that Garth would like what he was going to say. 'And yet some of these infidels are good, kind people. They did not treat me badly. It is a pity that they don't believe in the true God, but maybe they can't help it. They have been taught that their God is the right one.'

That sounded very bad to me. But the Spanish Friar did not sound as if he was angry with the infidels. I thought he sounded sad.

'Have you travelled to other shrines in England?' asked my Uncle Garth.

'I'm on my way now from Walsingham to Canterbury, but where I go hardly matters. That's not the point.'

'I never saw the point myself,' said Garth. 'It's simpler for me. Men grow corn and men must have bread. They need a miller to grind their corn and make their flour for them. Every day I know what I have to do. I walk to mass each Sunday as far as the church spire you see from the gate. That's as much of a pilgrim as I ever want to be.'

I was scared of speaking up in front of my uncle, but once again I had to know. I whispered to the Friar from my place at the foot of the step, where I sat with the cat on my knee, 'What is the point, please, holy Friar?'

He smiled at me, not at all angry that I had spoken. 'Perhaps there's none,' he said. 'Your uncle says men must eat. I bring you no food. I bring you nothing but words. But in every village and every farm I visited, from here to Jerusalem, I was offered food. I was given much more than food. We pilgrims want to get closer to God, perhaps, and we seek him in the shrines of his saints. The saints knew him better than we do. But there is something of God in every man, I think, and maybe that's all the point there is.'

That puzzled me. 'But what about the infidel?' I whispered, so Garth wouldn't hear me and say that I was rude. 'Isn't there something of God in him?'

'Of course not,' said my uncle impatiently. He had heard me after all. Then Edith called from the window, telling us to come in to supper.

CHAPTER FOUR

No one would have thought that my Uncle Garth would die before he was old. He was a big strong man. When I was a little child I believed that somehow his strength held up the mill. I was scared of him, but I would have been much more scared without him. I'll tell you how I first came to be with him.

I was very small when Garth first brought me to the mill. Perhaps I was two years old; I don't remember. When my mother died Uncle Garth came to fetch me. He carried me home in his arms. It was a night of bitter frost. As we walked through the wood I could hear the twigs snapping as they froze. No birds sang. When we got to the mill it was dark. Garth made the fire blaze. He put a bed for me in the corner close to the fire. I have slept there ever since.

That first night I lay watching the shadows of the flames on the wall, and the huge shadow of my uncle moving to and fro in front of the fire.

I suppose it was a strange life for a little child. But the kitchen was always warm, and there was always food. I ate what Garth ate. When I was still too small to sit up on a chair, he used to sit me on the table, and feed me porridge from his bowl. I can just remember that, but I must have got older very fast. I can't remember when I first looked round the mill. I've always known it as well as I know my own body.

Job was always there too. Job is my uncle's servant. He is just part of the mill. At night he goes home, but when I was young I never thought about him doing that. I just have that one picture of the first night, when everything in the shadows was still strange to me. But with my uncle there, I wasn't afraid.

I was no use to my uncle when I first came to the mill. I was hardly more than a baby. At night Garth had to put a napkin on me so I would not wet my bed. Every day he had to wash me, feed me and dress me. It was no task for a strong man. I think I understood this, because I very quickly learned to manage all these things for myself. I knew, even then, that I shouldn't put him to any trouble.

Only once did I ask for more than he could give me.

I can't remember all of it. I must have woken up in my bed by the kitchen hearth. Perhaps the fire was out, or the ashes had burned low. It was winter. I remember the dark pressing against my eyes. My blanket had fallen off and I was shivering. The wind howled round the house. It sounded like wolves outside in the yard. I was afraid of wolves. I had never seen one, but sometimes we could hear them howling in the woods on winter nights.

I would have been too scared to move if it had not been for the cat. The cat was sleeping on my bed. Somehow the cat had got into the middle of the bed, and I was pushed out against the cold stone wall. The cat had got the blanket.

I could feel the cat's warm fur in the dark. I heard her purr. I was cold and frightened, but the warm cat gave me courage. I picked up the cat. I was very small, and the cat was very heavy. I trod across the cold earth floor, holding the cat hard against my chest.

My uncle slept upstairs. The stone steps wound round and round in a spiral. A shaft of moonlight shone in through a little window at the top. The stone steps were like ice to my bare feet. I was so small I had to climb one step at a time. Because of the cat I couldn't steady myself with my hands. Clutching the heavy cat, I slowly climbed up to my uncle's door.

The door was shut. It had a big iron handle, but I was too small to reach up and turn it. I sat down on the icy step and wept. I clung to the warm furry cat for company, and I cried until Garth woke up. I heard the door open behind me. I heard Garth's voice speaking to me out of the dark. He picked me up. The cat leaped out of my arms and fled away down the stairs.

I clung to my uncle's shirt. I could feel the heat of his body through the coarse wool. He felt my cold feet, and cradled them in one of his big hands until they started to feel warm again. 'Now then, now then,' he said. 'This won't do. This won't do at all.'

That's all I remember. Knowing my uncle, I think he carried me back downstairs. Perhaps he tucked me up again in my place by the kitchen fire. Did he make sure I was warm? I can't remember.

I never went up that stair to his bedroom again. I grew up fast, and soon learned to be useful to him. I grew big enough to bring in wood and water. When I was tall enough I could stir the pot on the fire. As soon as I could be trusted with it, Garth gave me a knife. I learned to cut bread and meat, and chop the vegetables. I learned to weed the garden and sweep the floor. When Edith came to the mill, she took me in hand. I worked harder when she was there than I ever did when Garth and I were alone. In some ways it was worth it. Edith cooked good meals. Garth and I had never been well fed before.

The year the Spanish Friar came, I began my real work in the mill. That's where I got my strength, working in the mill. Now I can carry sacks of grain up to the top floor from one day's end to another. I can load a cart with sacks of flour in a few minutes. I was small for my age when I was a child, but because of the work I had to do I grew strong very quickly.

Until I could lift a sack of grain, I was not much use to my Uncle Garth. Even so, I was able to do many small jobs. Garth worked me hard, but he was fair. He was never cruel to me.

At first I was scared of the dark inside the mill. If you came into the mill from the bright sunshine outside you couldn't see anything at all. Even when you got used to the dark, you couldn't see into the corners. I used to think that something bad might lurk in the spaces where I couldn't see. But Uncle Garth had no time for nonsense like that. I knew that I had to get used to the mill. In fact before long I was happy there. Now I am happier in the mill than I am anywhere else in the world.

It was the noise that scared me to begin with. All day long we heard the rush of water outside, and the *clank-clank, clank-clank* of the great wheel going round. Indoors there was always the noise of stone grinding on stone, and the rattle of falling grain. We could not talk in ordinary voices. If we spoke we had to shout. The air was thick with flour dust. A visiting farmer would start to cough and choke in no time. I soon learned to be proud of the mill. Garth and I knew how to deal with it. I was proud of my work. I felt as if I belonged there. The mill was dark, dusty and noisy, but for me it was safe. It was my home.

Garth taught me to keep the mill clean. Every day I folded the empty sacks and put them away. Every day I coiled the string into neat balls. I swept the floor. I set the traps. Each day I went round and threw away the dead rats and mice. The cats helped us with the rats and mice. You couldn't keep a mill clean and safe without cats. If you had no cats, the rats and mice would eat the stored grain, and spread dirt all over the place. Cats are a miller's best friends.

Garth only beat me once. It was when he found me rolling in the flour bin. I jumped into the flour bin because I wanted to see how it felt to have flour all over me. It itched, and Garth beat me. I remember screaming and struggling, but I was not sorry. Garth made me scared though. I wasn't allowed to use the path by the big wheel, and after that beating I never dared to try. Before Edith came, a woman from the village used to cook our dinner for us twice a week. I think she was supposed to look after me. I have no picture of her in my mind. We had five cats, and their names were Moses, Bramble, Buttercup, Sukey and Aaron. Moses and Aaron were there when I came, but they didn't have any names before I knew them. The others were kittens born later.

I didn't like it when my Uncle

Garth starting going out in the evenings. All through one long summer he used to go out two or three times a week. I didn't like being left alone at the mill while the shadows began to lengthen. When Garth was not there I was afraid of the dark. I didn't know where he was. I had to go to bed by myself, and sometimes I wondered what I would do if he were still not there when the morning came. But he always was. He never said what he was doing. I was probably the last person in the valley to know that he was courting Edith.

I knew who she was, of course. She came with her parents and her brothers to church on Sundays. Sometimes Garth would speak to them after the service, while I waited at his side like a lost shadow. Sometimes Edith's brothers would tease me, and I would shrink back from them. I was always shy in company. Edith never took any notice of me at all.

Edith wasn't shy. Having all those brothers, she was used to men, and would talk to them boldly. She could look a man straight in the eye, and she never blushed or giggled like some girls do. You could tell that Garth liked her for that. She used to make him laugh, and then she would laugh with him, looking into his eyes. I'd never heard my uncle laugh so much before.

At my uncle's wedding I carried the sheaf of corn, which is supposed to bring children to a marriage. I wasn't sure I wanted Garth and Edith to have children. Sometimes I wonder if I brought bad luck to my uncle because of my bad thoughts on his wedding day. A big, kind man like Garth should have had a dozen sons and daughters to sit at the table on either side of him. But there was never any child but Joan.

He never laid a hand on Joan. He didn't spoil her though. Folk said he treated her too much like a boy, and that would be the ruin of her. By the time Joan was born I was nine years old and too big to be jealous of a baby. When she was ten she started working in the mill. I didn't mind much. I had grown up by then. I'd never expected Garth to pass on the mill to me. I was his sister's bastard child, and there was no reason why he should ever have taken me in. He did it because he had a good heart. He gave me a home and a place to earn my living. I never expected a share in the mill. Life was very different for Joan, of course, because she had a mother. But the cats were always mine, and no one has ever given them their names but me.

That one there, sitting on the bench beside you, he's Gato. Not the first Gato—that was his grandfather, but there's always been one called Gato, for the last twenty-two years. We just keep one tom cat. With so many kittens you have to drown some. I don't like drowning them. Someone has to do it though. I wouldn't expect Joan to do it. She wouldn't like that. I don't like doing it either, but that doesn't matter. It would be more cruel to let them starve.

CHAPTER FIVE

When my uncle died two years ago I was frightened. It happened all of a sudden. He went to work as he always did, and in the middle of the morning—we were grinding barley that day, it was November—he had a fit, and just dropped down dead. When Joan found him, the stones were grinding together without any grain. The big water wheel was still turning. I had to let go of my old idea that somehow my uncle *was* the mill. He and the mill had come into my life at the same time, you see, and I had always known them together. But very soon we were going on with our work as usual. Now Joan is the miller. Garth left the mill to her.

She isn't very big, my cousin Joan. Sometimes I think that little people aren't quite as real as big ones. There wouldn't be such a gap if they were gone. And yet I know that there's just as much soul in a small body. Joan is as much the mill as ever her father was. But she isn't strong in the way that Garth was. You never saw Garth the Miller? He was a big man, with very fair hair, though he was bald before he died. He had blue eyes that looked quite blank, but they weren't really. You couldn't put anything across on my uncle. Joan is just as clever, but then it was my Uncle Garth who taught her.

I take after my uncle, as you see. I'm not sure I ever loved him. We were too alike in some ways. The Spanish Friar was different. He was the first person I ever knew I loved.

Let me tell you about the Spanish Friar. That year when I was eight he stayed with us all winter. The people here used to flock to hear him. They came into the yard of the mill to listen to him. Sometimes when it was very cold Edith would let them into the kitchen, though not too near the fire. The Friar was an eye doctor as well as a Friar. People have a lot of trouble with their eyes in our valley. They used to come to him with toothache and sore joints as well, and he did what he could for them. But what he did best was tell stories.

No one had ever told me stories before. I used to get as close to the Friar as I could to listen. Most often I would have a cat or two curled up beside me. The Friar told stories about ordinary things. He talked about the mill and the woods and the farms, and the work people do in a village like ours. He used to tell stories out of the Bible as well. He used to make them sound ordinary too, as if they were about real people like us. When the people from the village were with us the Friar didn't talk very much about himself. Sometimes when they had gone away he used to answer my questions when I asked him about his own life, until Edith would stop me.

'Stop going on at him now,' she'd say, and she'd send me to fetch water, or feed the chickens, or take a message to my uncle. But in fact, I'm sure she wanted to hear as much as I did whatever the Friar had to say. I was useful to her, because she didn't want to have to ask for herself.

I remember one day the Friar was crushing a herb with a rounded stick, in a little bowl he had. I asked him what he was doing.

'I'm making a medicine from this herb. A lot of folk in this valley have bad eyes. This will make their eyes better.'

I looked at the green leaves in the bowl. He was crushing them to a juicy paste. 'What are the leaves?'

'They're called *eyebright*.' The Spanish Friar picked up a leafy stem from the table. It had a little blue and white flower. 'This is what eyebright looks like when it's growing.'

I took the plant from him. 'Eyebright,' I repeated. I looked at the little green leaves and the tiny flower. 'I've never seen it before,' I told him. 'I thought I knew all the plants that grow in our wood.'

'Ah, but this doesn't grow in your wood,' said the Friar. 'This grows on the mountains and the moors. It grows high up, in open places. That's what it likes. I picked it on a hillside two days' walk from here.'

I looked at the little flower. It had travelled much further than I had ever been. I wondered if I would ever go two days' walk away from the mill. I wondered if I would ever see the mountains and the moors that the Friar talked about.

'Why do you crush it with a stick in that bowl?' I asked.

'The stick is called a *pestle*,' said the Spanish Friar, 'and the bowl is called a *mortar*. A pestle and mortar is made for crushing herbs. I use mine to make medicine. Do you want to try it?'

I nodded.

The Friar gave me the pestle, and I began to crush the eyebright against the sides of the mortar.

'Are you going to give some eyebright to my Uncle Garth?' I asked the Friar.

'I don't think your uncle has sore eyes.'

'But it would make him see better,' I explained. 'He says it's because he's used to being in the dark mill. He can't see the bats flitting around the house at twilight. He can't see the fishes deep down in the mill pool. He can't see hazel nuts ripening on the tree. He says his eyes are getting old before their time. But you could give him eyebright and make them young again.'

'No,' said the Friar. 'Although I can cure many things, I can't give a man back the clear eyes of youth.

40

Look at the bats and the fishes and the nuts on the hazel tree while you can. Then, even if your eyes grow old before their time, you will always be able to remember these things.'

'I remember everything that happens,' I said proudly.

It was true that I remembered a great deal. But I don't remember everything.

I was clumsy when I first started helping the Friar to make his medicines. I soon learned though. After that day the Friar often let me help him when he was making medicines out of herbs.

One day we were putting chopped eyebright to soak in hot water. This was another way of making eye medicine. Edith was at the other end of the table, making bread. She was shaping the dough into round loaves, and putting them by the fire to rise. The kitchen was warm and smelled of yeast.

'Where did you live when you were

the same age as me?' I asked the Spanish Friar.

'Not in a mill,' he said. 'I lived in a village at the foot of the mountains. Where I grew up, the valleys are very steep. They have woods growing up their sides. The villages are in clearings high up above the river. Even higher than the village there are pastures where the cows and goats are put to graze. Above the pastures are the white crags of the mountains. Only the birds can reach the mountain tops. When I was the same age as you I was a boy herd. I looked after the cows in the high pasture.'

'Why did you go away?'

'When I was older, a Friar came to our village. He told stories, just as I tell you stories now. I listened to him. I wanted to go into the world that the stories belonged to, and so I left. I became a Friar too. I travelled far and wide. I was seeking always for the kingdom that he told us would come.'

I thought about that. I remembered what the Friar had told us before. He had said that he left his home to become a Friar because he thought it wrong that he had a good farm and plenty of money, when there were so many people in the world who had nothing. Now he seemed to be telling us a different story. He hadn't told us before that he was looking for a kingdom. 'Is this it here?' I asked him.

The Friar laughed. 'Yes and no,' he said, and I saw Edith smile. 'The kingdom that he spoke of is not of this world. Many men have died trying to make that kingdom come. I am not so brave, and so I travel about and tell people stories. But even though I am not as brave as many of my brothers, I get a glimpse sometimes of what that Friar was talking to us about.'

I thought that over. 'Why did they die?'

He told me about the holy saints then. In the evenings that followed he told us many stories about saints who had lived long ago. Some of them had died in horrible ways. The night after the Friar told us about Saint Lawrence I had a bad dream. Saint Lawrence lived in Rome a long time ago. In those days you were not allowed to be a Christian in Rome. The Emperors, who were infidels, killed all the Christians they could. The saints who were killed were holy martyrs. I would hate to be a holy martyr. To be honest with you, I think I would rather be an infidel. I see no point in dying for nothing. There is always something worth living for, however little, or so I think.

Saint Lawrence was willing to be a martyr. He could have just kept quiet, which is what I would have done. But he kept saying out loud what he thought, and so they killed him. They roasted him on a griddle over a fire. He burned very slowly, but he still would not say that he wasn't a Christian. In the end he died. While the Friar told us the story I looked into our kitchen fire. We have a big iron griddle that goes right over the fire. The griddle is like a big tray with holes in it for the heat to get through. You can put pans on it to boil, or loaves to bake, or meat and fish to roast. That evening we had finished our meal, and I had put hazel nuts from my store to roast on the griddle. As the flames licked gently round the nuts, the shells turned dark brown and then black. At last the nuts split open and you could see the sweet flesh inside. In winter we often roast nuts on the griddle. They taste very good.

I watched the hazel nuts slowly roasting. I saw them crack open one by one. Instead of making my mouth water, as it usually did, the sight of the roasting nuts made me feel cold and sick. When the story was finished, I still didn't see the point. I didn't see how a holy saint suffering like that had done anyone any good.

That night I dreamed that the mill was being burned down, and I was trapped in the middle of it. I woke up in terror. I stared at the embers of the fire until I remembered where I was. I sat up and saw the Spanish Friar sleeping at the other side of the hearth. He lay on his back with his mouth a little open. He looked very peaceful, as if he were not dreaming at all. I wanted to crawl in beside him. I wanted to take comfort from his warmth. But I would never have dared to do such a thing. I watched him for a long time. In the end I must have gone to sleep again.

That was the first bad dream. Others followed. I used to dream about Edith. I dreamed once that I was killing her. I was mashing her to a pulp with a huge pestle and mortar. Another time I was hitting her with my fists until her blood ran. In the morning I was always ashamed, although nothing had really happened. I used to watch her, though, and say less than usual. Perhaps that was why she took to sending me on errands.

I don't mean she just sent me to collect eggs, or do any of the jobs I had been doing since I could be of any use at all. I mean long errands. Once she sent me down to the village to fetch a goose. Another day she told me to go to the smithy to ask if we might bring the pony tomorrow. The smith was as surprised as I was.

'You know very well you can come by any time you like,' he said to me. He thought that I was telling a lie about Edith sending me. Most children like to get inside the smithy. I wanted to tell him that if anyone was making up stories, it was not I. I dared not say it. The smith was a good friend of my uncle's. He would have told my uncle if he thought I was cheeky. But all through

November and December I was sent on one message after another. I began to think it was very unfair.

When the weather was bad Edith couldn't send me out. One day I was sitting at the kitchen table. I was cross. I knew I was not wanted and I was glad to be there, getting in her way. The Friar was at home too. The rain lashed down outside. A few drops came flying down the chimney. They hissed into the fire. Edith gave me onions to chop. My eyes smarted, and I dripped sore tears on to the knife. The Friar and Edith were quiet at first, and then they began to talk as if I were not there.

'Wasn't it difficult, though,' Edith was saying, 'knowing you'd never even find out? I don't think I could make up my mind to that.'

'If you were called to make that vow, you would do it. But you're a married woman, that's your part in life. Mine is different.'

'But don't you ever wonder? I

mean, you must wonder what it would be like to go with a woman?'

The Spanish Friar didn't answer at once. He let Gato jump up on his knee, and stroked him so that the cat purred loudly. 'No,' he said. 'It isn't that I wonder.'

Edith gave him a strange look. 'You mean it isn't quite like that?'

'Not quite as you think, no.'

It didn't mean a thing to me. I couldn't understand what they were talking about, but I watched their faces. In particular I looked at the Spanish Friar. His face was not like any other face that I knew. It wasn't just that he was darker than we were. It was that I could see more feelings in his face than I could see in other people's. I didn't know what the feelings were, but I could see them. I could see more light and shade. His face next to my uncle's was like a day of sun and wind next to a day of clouds. With my uncle I never knew what he was feeling about anything. I loved the Spanish Friar for showing his feelings in his face, even though I didn't understand what it was that the feelings were about.

At night I lay on my mattress and he lay on his, one on each side of the kitchen fire. The cats were always curled up on the hearth between us. I shut my eyes tight and thought about the Spanish Friar. I imagined those dark eyes looking into mine quite tenderly. I had never seen anyone's eyes look tender, so far as I could remember. But I found that I could picture what it might be like. A tender look, is, I think, one where the person's eyes aren't quite focussed. The gates to the mind are open, with no guards to stop you looking in. If someone were to look at me tenderly, it would be like looking into the spaces between the ordinary person that I usually see. It would be like looking into a shadowy inside, which a sensible person is usually careful to hide.

I knew nothing about touching. I knew that I would like the Spanish Friar to touch me, but I didn't know how that would happen. I knew about sex, of course. The cats do it all the time. It is quite short, and at the end the female yowls as if she is in pain. A cat cannot tell you whether it is in pain or not. I knew what it was that my uncle the miller and Edith did when they lay together in bed. Of course I never saw them there. I didn't know how often it happened. I didn't know what it was like for either of them.

Sometimes in the kitchen my Uncle Garth would lay his hand on Edith's shoulder as he passed her when she was working at the table. Sometimes when he did that she would turn round and smile. Before the Spanish Friar came, I slept alone in the kitchen. When I was little I felt left out because my uncle and his wife lay together up the stairs and never wanted me.

51

So I didn't know very much. But I used to think how it would be to curl up against the warmth of the Spanish Friar. My uncle was warm. When I was a baby, and he carried me home through the wood, and the trees were stiff with frost around us, I was warm against his chest. Sometimes when I was small Garth carried me on his back. As far as I remember Garth only once held me in his arms. I would have liked the Spanish Friar to hold me in his arms. I shut my eyes tightly, alone on my mattress, and pretended that it was so. But I didn't know enough. I wanted something else in my picture, but I didn't know what it was. I could see an empty space in my mind, but I couldn't see any way to fill it.

CHAPTER SIX

In the end my dream came true. But when it did, it didn't make me happy. I didn't like it at all, and at the end I felt more alone than I had ever felt before.

Above the mill we have a big mill pond. When the mill isn't working the mill pond is very still. Sometimes when I was little I used to gaze into the mill pond, watching the little fishes flashing to and fro down there in the dark. If I stopped looking at the fishes I'd look at the surface of the water instead. Then I'd see myself reflected in the water. It was the only time I ever saw my own face.

But then my uncle used to open the sluice gates. When he did that, white water poured out of the pond. There would be a great rushing sound, and slowly the big wheel would start to turn. Instead of peace and stillness there would be clanking and grinding. Instead of seeing my face mirrored in the water, I'd see the currents making ripples that went faster and faster as I watched. That was what it was like with the Spanish Friar, when at last it really happened.

There was an oak tree just a little way inside our wood. It had big branches that stuck out sideways. That winter, when I was eight years old, the branches grew just close enough for me to be able to climb them. One day I climbed up into the tree just as the dusk was falling. There was a branch that I liked to sit on. I could lean back against the trunk and watch the world below.

It was December, and the day was dwindling into dark. The fallen leaves and withered bracken glowed like fire. It seemed as if they held their own light inside them. Two deer bounded past below me with a faint thud of hooves. An owl flew by me, very low, and I jumped. It flew as silently as the dark, which came creeping in behind it. A shiver of cold ran through the leaves that still clung to the branches. The first touch of night nipped my face and toes. It was time to climb down. I stayed, because the evening held me.

I saw two people among the fallen leaves. They looked like ghosts. They seemed all grey. I was frightened. I lay flat against my branch, but they never looked up. A gust of wind blew over me. A shower of rain came with it. The two people turned their backs to the wind. They ran across the leaves into the shelter of my tree.

I recognised Edith by her red shawl. The man with her wore a long brown robe tied with a white cord at his waist. He pushed back the hood of his robe. It was the Spanish Friar. I think perhaps I made a sound, but the wind stopped them from hearing me. The dead leaves rustled in the wind. Edith was gripping the Friar's arm. She was speaking to him very fast. I couldn't hear what she said. Her other hand was waving about, the way it does when she's excited. The Friar laid his hand over hers, where she was holding his sleeve. Edith said something that might have been a sob, and hid her face with her other arm.

The Spanish Friar was always gentle. He never even pushed a cat off a bench when he wanted to sit down. He always lifted it up carefully, and settled it down, still curled up, on his knee. I have never known anyone else treat a cat that way. But now the Friar was being fierce and sudden. I was shocked. I was very scared as well.

I clutched my branch as if that could comfort me. The world suddenly seemed to be spinning round me. I felt as if I was in danger and might fall, even though I was safe on my big branch. I saw the

Friar pull Edith's arm away from her face, and force her into his arms.

I couldn't see Edith's face. The Friar's head hid her from me. From up above I could see the bald top of his head where the hair was shaved off. His hair was shaved like that to show he was a Friar. It was a sign that he was holy. My legs felt weak, though I kept my grip on the tree. My stomach felt hot. The bark of the oak was rough under my cold hands. I rubbed my wet palms against it. The wood was knobbly and cold, but I was sweating. I saw Edith's hands grip the Friar's shoulders. Then I saw her arms twined around his neck. Her hood fell back. I could see her hair coming loose and falling down on her shoulders. I had never seen her hair loose before. It was very thick and curly. With her hair undone she looked like a girl and not like a married woman.

There was a stabbing pain in the pit of my stomach. I felt sick. My arms and legs felt loose as if I were about to fall. But my branch was wide and flat on top the way an old oak is, and it held me safe. I pressed my cheek against the wood, and shut my eyes.

When I looked again they were not there. The rain was falling gently. It sounded like the stream flowing past the mill on a calm evening. Dark was filling up the space below the trees. I had to wait a long time before I was steady enough to climb down. The oak tree seemed like a big comforting friend. It would have held me safe for a hundred years if I had needed it.

CHAPTER SEVEN

I lose track of time when I think about that winter. I only remember feeling scared and anxious all the time. The pain under my ribs didn't go away. I spent my time watching them. I was always watching. Nothing seemed safe any more. I felt as if the mill might come suddenly tumbling round my ears. Every change of wind or weather seemed dangerous.

We sat at the table every evening at supper: Garth, Edith, myself and the Spanish Friar. My uncle never sat up late. When he and Edith had gone to bed, the Friar and I brought out our mattresses and lay down. The Friar still told stories. In the daytime the people still came to hear him. Sometimes he went out, leaving us all at home, and that was safer.

Because I had a secret I felt as if I had done something wrong. At night I thought about how I had lain on my branch in the oak tree. I remembered the feel of the bark under my hands. I remembered how my legs had twined around the branch. I remembered the hot pang in my stomach. I thought about it so much that I kept feeling it all over again. I tried to stop thinking about the oak tree.

That was worse. If I didn't think about the oak tree any more, I found myself thinking about the Spanish Friar instead. I thought about his body. I knew somehow that he would feel warm. His skin under the robe must be brown like his hands. I thought that he would be as soft as a cat. He would be gentle but also fierce. I had seen him being fierce when he forced Edith into his arms. I went over that memory again and again. I thought about it carefully

60

because I didn't want to get it wrong in my mind. I did not want to wear the memory out.

So I would roll over on to my back, and listen for the Friar's breathing in the dark. If I heard him stir or mutter my mouth would go dry. My legs would ache for his warmth. I was closer to him than Edith was when we lay on our mattresses at night. I had him to myself alone. She lay upstairs, doing whatever she did with my Uncle Garth at night. She and Garth were up there in the big bed that I had never seen unmade.

Christmas came and went. After Twelfth Night—the last night of Christmas—my uncle took some flour up to the bakery in the town. It was like spring, even though it wasn't. A pale sun shone in the January sky. There were icicles in the hedges where the bramble berries had been. The road was frozen hard, and that was why Garth seized the chance to go. If the ice melted there would be too much mud to get the cart along the road. The mill pond was frozen over, and the mill was shut up. There was nothing to stay for, and so Garth left. I shall never know now what he thought. His face never changed. Perhaps if I had not been there he would have taken Edith with him.

Garth was hardly ever away. I didn't feel safe in the mill without him. That night I was very glad of the Friar on his mattress beside me. I would have been scared to be alone. I fell asleep to the mutter of his voice praying. He did this every night. A Friar has to say prayers at certain times of the day and night. The Spanish Friar never forgot to do this, so far as I know. I had got used to hearing him pray. It wasn't like listening to him telling a story. He said the words to himself alone, just as he would have done if I had not been there.

When I woke the embers of the

fire were glowing on the hearth. Cats' eyes gleamed in the dark. I listened for the Friar's breathing. I heard only silence. I strained my ears, and the silence seemed to roar inside my head. My stomach felt cold.

I did what I had never dared to do before. I crawled out of my bed and over to his. I felt his cold blanket and the flat mattress on the floor. A bitter wind drove through my shirt. My skin prickled. What I did next wasn't brave. I was so scared and upset that I would have done anything. I stood up, felt my way to the table, and found the lamp. It was full to the brim with oil. I took the tongs from the hearth, and used them to pick up a burning ember. My hands shook as I held the coal to the wick of the lamp. I got the lamp lit.

I went to the door and up the stone stairs. The stone was like ice to my bare feet. I hardly seemed to feel it. I crept to the door of my uncle's room. A black shadow slipped up the stairs before me. It pressed and rubbed against the closed door. When it turned I saw a white front and whiskers. It was the kitten I had called Gato.

I stood at the top of the stair. The door handle was under my hand. The iron ring was so cold it felt hot. I gripped it and turned it. I turned it so slowly it hardly seemed to move. I was scared that it would make a noise. I had laid my lamp on the top step. The wind made the flame flutter. I bit my lip and kept turning the iron ring. Then I pushed the door, slow and hard.

It opened just a little bit. The wind howled through the crack. I gasped with cold. The lamp went out. The wind was moaning like a hurt child. I stared into nothing. Then I saw the dark coming out of the room at me. It was going to swallow me up. I beat on the dark with my fists and screamed for it to let me go. I'd heard the crying in the wind before. I knew that I had been in this same place before, and that it had been waiting to get me again, all this time.

The Friar was there. I was in his arms. It was not my fault. He was naked. His skin was warm against mine, soft as a cat. But when I rubbed my face against his, his cheek was rough. It prickled me. I felt his hands clasp me through my thin shirt. I went limp against him, just like in my dream.

'For God's sake, what is it?' The voice from inside the room was high and frightened. 'Is it the cat?'

I had forgotten about my aunt. Her voice jarred me. It broke my dream into little pieces. The Spanish Friar was touching my face, but only to make sure who I was.

'No, it's the child.'

'The child?' There was a note of horror in the shrill voice.

'Hush, it won't mean anything.' He was still holding me. 'Are you all right? What is it?'

When I spoke I could hear that I was crying. 'You were gone.'

'And that worried you? But look, I've not gone far. Don't be upset. I'll take you back. Wait there.'

I was left standing in the cold, the dark all round me. I heard my aunt whispering, but the Spanish Friar answered her out loud. 'There's no harm done. The child's a restless sleeper. In the morning it'll all be forgotten, another bad dream. I'll make sure it's all right. Don't worry.'

There was a pause. I heard more whispers. Then he was back. He picked me up, and I felt the rough wool of his robe. 'Poor little shrimp,' he said. 'You're frozen. You should stay in bed on a night like this or you'll catch your death.'

We were going down the stairs now. It was bumpy being carried in his arms like a baby. I wriggled. 'Keep still. You're too heavy.' He pushed the kitchen door open. The firelight made the room seem quite light after the dark stair. He dumped me back on my bed and pulled the cover up. I think he would have gone but I grabbed his sleeve.

'What is it?'

I might have said I loved him. I might have said something which I would burn with shame to think of now. I might have cried. Thank God I caught the note of impatience in his voice. He was probably cold too, poor man. Wherever he wanted to be, it wasn't with me. He had told my aunt it would be all right. But he must have been worrying about what would happen next. I heard all that in his voice. Suddenly I thought of my Uncle Garth. Garth's face never showed how he felt to anyone. I had never heard fear in Garth's voice, and I never would. I felt proud of Garth. I was glad that he was my uncle. 'I want the cat.' I said. I sounded very sulky. That way I kept my pride.

'The cat?'

'Gato. Gato was on the stairs.' I suddenly realised that I could help him. I could get the Spanish Friar and Edith out of trouble. I could get them, and myself, out of the whole situation. I had the power to save us. The Spanish Friar and Edith couldn't make everything all right, but I could. 'I was looking for the cat.'

'It was the cat you were after?'

'Yes.'

He took the lamp and went out. Two minutes later he was back. He held Gato under the belly, so that the cat curved over his hand like a sleek black snake. Gato was born here at the mill. He was afraid of nothing, because no one had ever frightened him. That was why you could hold him any way you liked and he would just flop.

'Here's your cat. Will you be all right now?'

'Yes.' I scooped Gato up into my

arms. Then I laid him down beside me in my bed.

The Spanish Friar stood over me, holding the lamp. I had never seen him look worried before. He cleared his throat. 'You must have wondered where I was.'

I stroked my cat.

'The shutter was jammed. Your uncle can shift it, but it was too hard for Edith. The wind was coming right through. Your aunt wanted the shutter closed.'

I looked away.

'So you won't be frightened now?'

I looked at him and shook my head. I think he went upstairs again, but not for long. I heard him come in and lie down. I listened to his breathing and I could tell that he was not asleep.

Gato stretched himself against me and dug in his claws. I unhooked him gently, and laid him across my chest.

CHAPTER EIGHT

So that's it. I've never told my story before to anyone. But you asked about my cousin Joan. Joan owns the mill now. We work here together. She needs my help to run the place. She knows she can trust me. Ever since she was a little girl she has known that I would look after her. I used to carry her when she was a baby. She was as safe in my arms as a baby owl in its nest in the oak tree. I love Joan in the same way as I loved the Spanish Friar. I would do anything in the world to keep her safe.

I've never said so to her. She would hate to hear that sort of talk from me. I've never talked to her about the Spanish Friar. Perhaps she doesn't even know that he was here.

She was born at harvest time, and by that time the Spanish Friar was long gone. Edith has never spoken of him. I'm not usually one to talk, anyway.

The Spanish Friar was a man, and much older than me. Joan is a girl, and she is younger. I don't know where that leaves me. I say I loved them both. Love is a difficult thing.

The mill is all I have. It's not mine. My uncle is dead now, but from the day he brought me here, I knew where I belonged. I'm the only one left that takes after him. I don't know where he is now.

There is a picture of heaven on the wall inside our church. That's the church whose spire you see from our gate. I suppose the picture is telling the truth, and that is what heaven is like. I like to think there is a space between that kingdom and this one here on earth. I like to think there is a gate between heaven and earth that a man can sometimes look through. If Garth were peeping through that gate to see what is happening here, he wouldn't be looking for me. It would be Joan that Garth would look for. Garth loved his daughter Joan. He didn't understand her very well. They were not at all like one another. But if Garth were ever to take his eyes from Joan, and notice me, he might be glad to know that I'm still here in the old place. I think I owe him that.